The Boy Who Saw
BIGFOOT

Weekly Reader Books presents

The Boy Who Saw
BIGFOOT

Marian T. Place

DODD, MEAD & COMPANY
NEW YORK

Library of Congress Cataloging in Publication Data

Place, Marian Templeton.
The boy who saw Bigfoot.

SUMMARY: A ten-year-old boy, placed once again
with new foster parents, becomes involved in a search
for Bigfoot.
[1. Sasquatch—Fiction. 2. Foster home care—
Fiction. 3. Washington (State)—Fiction. 4. Forests
and forestry—Fiction] I. Title.
PZ7.P69Bp   [Fic]   78-23199
ISBN 0-396-07644-0

To Amy

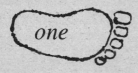

one

MY NAME IS Joey Wilson. I am ten, and live in a foster home in the mountains of western Washington. My foster mother's name is Sara Brown. The story I am going to tell happened to her and me both. I got my name and picture in the newspapers, and on television, and in *The Weekly Reader*. Sara didn't. She told those reporters and cameramen, "You leave me out of this. It's Joey's story."

It isn't all my story. Without Sara I never would have tried to make friends with the hairy monster called Bigfoot. If you saw me on television, you would think that I just walked in the woods one day, and *bam!* there was Bigfoot! The trouble with television is you get only two or three minutes to talk. No way can you tell the whole story that fast.

Here is my story from the beginning.

First I want to explain something. I did not ask to live with Sara and Mike Brown. The caseworker lady at the county Children's Services office placed me there. Yeah, *placed.* That's the right word.

Sara and Mike had raised four kids. After they grew up and left home, Sara got lonesome. Mike drives a logging truck. He leaves for work at daylight, six days a week. Sara doesn't sit around all day drinking coffee and watching television. She doesn't have neighbors because the Browns live in the mountains, near logging camps. Sara doesn't fuss much with keeping house, either. The things she likes best are fishing and hiking. Only, Mike would not let her go alone anymore. So that is why Sara asked the caseworker, Mrs. Adams, "Can some boy who likes to fish come to live with us?"

Mrs. Adams answered, "Yes. In fact, right now I am trying to find a home for a boy nobody wants. Let me tell you about him." She said that nobody knows who my folks are, or where they are. My mother joined a group of hippies who lived on a farm. She told them her name was Mary Wilson, but it wasn't. After I was born, she went away without saying good-bye.

The hippies took care of me until they got arrested for growing marijuana. I was three years old then, and afraid of strangers. None of the hippies claimed me. Right then was when I became a problem, even though it wasn't my fault. The problem was that someone had to look after me. A judge made me a ward of the court. That way there was money from the county Children's Services fund to pay someone to do it. So that's how I got placed in a foster home. I cried so much the foster mother made Mrs. Adams place me somewhere else. After that, I got placed in a different home about every six months, or a year, because I was hard to handle. The foster parents told Mrs. Adams I had awful tantrums. I cussed, and snitched money, and fibbed, and broke windows, and ran away a lot.

This was true. A guy will pull lots of tricks to get attention. The first time I ran away, I thought my foster parents would miss me. When I came back, I didn't get hugs and kisses. I got larruped. So I did other things to get even. Finally, even though foster parents got paid over one hundred dollars a month to look after me, nobody wanted me.

I didn't care. I got used to being traded in like a used car. I just told myself, "Tough luck, kid. Keep your fingers crossed. The next place will be lots better."

You can guess what happened. The next place wasn't lots better, nor the ones after that. But I kept hoping someday I'd have a home with real parents, not the kind who got paid to look after me. Sure, I dreamed about being placed in a millionaire's home, or with a family of circus performers, or one of those family singing groups you see on television. But I told myself, "Things like that only happen to winners." That left me out.

Anyhow, after Mrs. Adams told Sara why nobody wanted me, Sara told her, "I want him. You tell that boy Joey he is welcome at our house. Bring him out as soon as you can."

Later that afternoon Mrs. Adams drove out to where I was staying at the Halfway House. It's just what it is called—a house for kids and grownups who are halfway between where they don't want to be anymore, and not yet where they want to be pretty soon.

First thing Mrs. Adams said was, "I think I found a nice home for you, Joey. A lady came to the office. She asked if some boy who liked to fish could come and live with her and her husband. I said yes, you could. You do like to fish, don't you?"

I made a dopey face. How would I know if I like to fish? Nobody ever took me.

"The lady's name is Sara Brown. She and her husband, Mike, live out in the country. You'd like to live out in the country, wouldn't you? It would be a nice change. You might be very happy living out in the country."

You probably guessed I am a city kid. But I know what trees look like. I've seen lots of logging trucks hauling big logs on the highway near my school. But to be truthful, I don't know straight up about the country. I didn't give a hang where these folks lived, and said so.

Mrs. Adams said, "Please try to be good, Joey."

What I wanted to say was, "Well, how about this Sara Brown? Did you tell her to be good? Why does it always got to be me?" But I kept my mouth shut. If I didn't like living at Sara's house, I would run away again. Being a runaway in summer is not so bad. So, I packed my sack, and drove with Mrs. Adams to my new foster mother's place.

It was early June, and not raining for a change. We drove past small farms and two sawmills. One cut cedar shingles for roofs. The other produced fence posts and railroad ties. Then the road followed a river through the forest. There were fishing resorts and campgrounds along the river. Next we turned off and drove alongside a creek, and more campgrounds. The trees were so tall I could not see the sky.

Finally we stopped in front of a log cabin. I was glad to see a television antenna on the roof. I watch a lot of television day and night. Foster mothers let me watch all I want. Then they know where I am, and what I am doing.

Mrs. Adams marched me up on the porch. The door was open so she called, "Yoo-hoo, Mrs. Brown, here we are."

I heard heavy footsteps. Then Sara appeared . . . all six feet of her. I don't mean she had six feet. She was six feet tall. She was wearing a man's red plaid shirt, jeans, and laced boots. Her black hair was pulled back into a braid. No kidding, her hands were as big as my feet!

I didn't say hello, or anything. I was scared stiff. I have been swatted enough to be an expert on lickings. I figured right then and there I would be mighty careful how close I got to Sara.

"Glad you got here," she said. "It's hot inside. Let's sit out here to talk."

We sat on the top step, with Sara in the middle. Sara told me straight out how things were going to be. All I had to do was fish and hike with her. I didn't have to haul kindling for the woodstove, or

12

weed the garden, or feed the chickens. But I did have to brush my teeth every day. "No brushing, no fishing. Understand?"

I nodded. My stomach was so tied up in knots that I could not answer out loud.

Mrs. Adams started to talk. I tuned her out, and looked around. That made me more scared than ever. As I said before, I don't know anything about the country. A few times I got to go to a summer camp program in the city park. From Sara's front step all I could see was the road, the electric power line, woods and more woods, and a snow-covered mountain in the distance. No cars, no people, no stores, nothing but woods. They would be real scary at night. When I got ready to run away, I would have to do it in the daytime.

A big yellow cat jumped up on the step. Darned if he didn't come right up to me, and rub his ears on my ankle. When I scratched his ears, he purred real loud. Then he hopped in my lap.

I butted in on the ladies' talk. "Hey, Sara, can I have this cat? He likes me!"

Sara answered, "You'll have to ask the cat. If it's all right with him, it's all right with me."

Now that was a crazy answer. Ask a cat a question? I said, "Oh, yeah?"

"Yeah."

I looked that cat square in the eye, and talked to him. It was fun, especially when he answered with a "meow."

Sara stood up. From where I was sitting, she looked ten feet tall. "Come on, Joey. I will show you where you are going to sleep."

I asked if I could bring the cat.

Mrs. Adams said, "Maybe Mrs. Brown doesn't allow cats in her house."

Sara winked at me. "Mrs. Adams doesn't know much about cats, does she?"

I wanted to say, "She doesn't know much about kids, either." But I didn't. No use getting into trouble right away for being sassy. I carried that big yellow cat like he was a baby. He didn't even open his eyes. We followed Sara inside. On the left was the living room. It had a real fireplace, some lumpy chairs, a big lamp, and piles of books and magazines on the floor. There was another cat curled up on top of the television set.

On the other side of the room was a round dining table and chairs. Beyond that was a kitchen with another bare table in the center. The cookstove was the old-fashioned kind that burned wood. There was a box of kindling next to it. Behind that was another box with kittens curled up in it. Next we stepped into a hall. It led to three bedrooms and a bathroom.

Sara explained, "Mike and I sleep here. My girls had this room with the flowered curtains. The boys used this one with the bunk beds."

In the boys' room I spied a wall lamp over the lower bunk and a pile of comic books on the floor. "Do I sleep here?"

Sara smiled, "Yup."

I looked around like maybe I had just landed on another planet. I never had a room all to myself, ever. I never had a pile of comic books all to myself, either. "Can the cat sleep with me? What's his name?"

The cat's name was Bingo. He could sleep with me.

Sara told me to make myself at home. She was going to start fixing supper. "Do whatever you feel like doing until Mike gets home. Okay?"

It was okay.

Mrs. Adams said, "Good-bye, Joey. Be a good boy."

I nodded.

"I'll be seeing you."

She would, too. She had to check up on me every

month. Also, she would see me when Sara and Mike got tired of having me around. That always happened. It would take me a while to know when might be a good time to run away from this new place.

two

SARA HAD TOLD me I could make myself at home. So I did, or tried to. I put Bingo on the bed. There was a hairbrush on the dresser, so I brushed him. He liked that. Then I picked up a comic book and stretched out on the lower bunk. But I could not read. My stomach felt like it was full of rocks. It hurt! It gets that way whenever I move to a new place.

Just then Sara appeared in the doorway. She had my sack of stuff. "Put your things in the dresser drawers when you feel like it. Would you like a glass of milk?"

I made a face. "I hate milk. Have you got any pop?"

There was no pop. Also, there was no corner

store where I could go buy some. I had money in my jeans. I always have money. One foster mother paid me to stay out of sight! The last one kept all the money the county paid her, and spent it on herself. So I snitched whenever I wanted some.

"I'll be in the kitchen," Sara said, and went there.

That hurt in my stomach was so bad I had to do something. I went into the kitchen and said I would drink a glass of milk.

"Help yourself." Sara didn't pour the milk because her hands were full. I did, and didn't make a mess. Then I watched Sara. She was doing something I had never seen anybody do, except on television and in schoolbook pictures. She was kneading bread dough. Then she pulled off bits, and rounded them into loaves. Next she plopped them into bread pans. There was still dough left over. She rolled it out, buttered the top, and sprinkled brown sugar and cinnamon on it.

"Do you like raisins?" she asked.

"Yeah. They're okay."

She handed me a bag of raisins. "Sprinkle some on, will you, while I grease the pan for the rolls?"

I wiped my hands on my jeans and sprinkled raisins. Then I helped Sara roll up the dough, and cut it into separate rolls.

"The bread and rolls have to rise now. Why don't you walk around outside? I'll call you when they are baked."

When I went out the back door, the hinge squeaked. Quick as a flash, Bingo squeezed through a hole in the screen. We walked around together. The yard was full of neat stuff. Some folks would call it junk, but not me. I found boards, and wire, old tires, bits of machinery, lots of things. I looked for a hammer and nails so I could build something. I got so interested wondering what to build that I forgot about my stomach ache.

Sara hollered through the open kitchen window. "Rolls are done!"

Boy! Can she holler! But she wasn't mad. I ran inside. She was frosting hot cinnamon rolls, and handed me one. I nibbled the edges, and got frosting on my nose. "That's the best cinnamon roll I ever ate. Hey, can I frost the rest of them?"

"Sure. But you'll have to lick the knife and bowl clean afterwards."

I did what she said.

Pretty soon there was this loud noise and the

windows rattled. A huge logging truck rolled past the kitchen window.

"That's Mike. You better go say hello to him."

I ran outside. I am used to logging trucks because where I live is logging country. Mike turned off the motor, and climbed down out of the cab. Golly, he was taller than Sara!

"Hi, Joey. Glad you got here all right." There was none of this fakey business of shaking hands, or saying we'd be pals. "What have you been doing?"

"Helping Sara. Hey, you know what? I helped make cinnamon rolls, and then frosted them! All by myself!"

Mike leaned over so he could look me in the eye. "Thanks, fella. I sure appreciate your giving Sara a hand. After supper I have to change the oil on this rig. You want to help?"

I sure did. It was a big job. By the time we finished, it was bedtime. Not for me. For Mike. I am used to staying up until after the late-late television movie was over. "Does everybody go to bed now?"

Mike yawned. "Yup. You can read if you want."

There was no television or radio in my bedroom. I called it that already. I sure as heck wasn't going to sit up all by myself in a strange house. "Okay."

Mike, not Sara, showed me which was my towel rack in the bathroom, and where to hang my toothbrush. I told him, "Sara said I had to brush my teeth, or I couldn't go fishing."

"That's the rule. She makes me do that. All our kids had to do that."

So I brushed. I didn't need help getting into bed, but do you know what happened? First, Mike asked me if I had a pretty good day. Well, I had, to tell the truth. "Real good."

"It was good for us, too, Joey. We like having a boy around the house again." Then he kissed me goodnight! "See you in the morning?"

"See you in the morning," I promised. And I meant it. I didn't think once about running away. I turned the light out and went right to sleep.

The next morning I woke up early because I was so hungry. Bingo was gone. I crawled out of the bunk and tiptoed into the kitchen. It sure was quiet. No radio or TV squawking, no babies crying, no kids fighting over cereal boxes. I could hear the wood burning in the stove, and the coffeepot perking.

Mike was there. He whispered, "We've got to be quiet. Sara is asleep."

"Are you cooking breakfast?" I never knew a man to do that.

"Sure. Why not?" He loaded a plate with hotcakes and bacon. "Sit down. The syrup is in that brown bottle."

I really like syrup. "Can I have all I want?"

"Help yourself."

"Can I have coffee with canned milk and sugar? I hate milk."

"Sure, but do me a favor. Sara made our kids drink a glass of milk every day. You know how mothers are. They're strong on things like brushing teeth and drinking milk. Drink one glass a day for her. Then you can have all the coffee you want."

I didn't know how mothers are, but I could do that much for Sara. Mike sat down to eat. Every time I finished a hotcake, he slid another one on the plate. When we finished, he put the dishes and mugs in the sink. I never saw a man do that before, either.

Sara had packed Mike's lunch bucket the night before. He tucked it under his arm, gave me a hug, and headed for the back door. "You take good care of Sara today. Promise?"

I promised.

After Mike drove off, I was puzzled. Anyone as big as Sara didn't need a half-pint-sized kid looking after her. There had to be some reason. I could not figure it out. I would have to wait until the answer hit me in the head.

While I was sitting at the table, Bingo climbed in through the hole in the screen door. He jumped up on my lap, and started to purr. I call that "talking." So, I asked Bingo how to take good care of Sara. He told me. Don't laugh! He did! He started to wash his ears. That gave me an idea. My ears were clean, but the dishes in the sink weren't. I washed them, and wiped the table clean.

Sara was so surprised she gave me a hug. I tried to duck, but found she could hug a guy without breaking his ribs.

Afterwards we poked around in her boys' closet. We could not find any fishing boots or a jacket small enough for me. When Sara saw how few clothes I had, and only worn tennis shoes, she got awfully red in the face. See, part of the money paid to a foster parent is supposed to be spent on clothes and toys. The last foster mother I had before Sara spent all the money in taverns. I never tattled on her. Nobody ever believed anything I said anyway.

Sara said, "Come on. We're going to town and

get you some clothes. We'll go fishing when we get back."

Sara drives an old four-wheel-drive jeep station wagon. It needed gasoline so she filled the tank from a big one at the back of their place. There was another tank, three times bigger, for storing diesel oil to run the logging truck.

I soon found out that riding in the jeep was like riding a bucking bronc. I know what that is like because once, at a day camp, I got bucked off a pony. I didn't cry, either. Anyhow, I hung onto the jeep seat all the way to town. The windows were open so it was too noisy to talk. Sara took me to J.C. Penney's and bought a big pile of things: underwear, socks, jeans, plaid shirts like hers and Mike's, a rainproof jacket, new tennis shoes, a fishing hat, fishing boots and real hiking boots.

I was worried sick. "Sara, if you pay for this, you won't get your money back until next month. The check won't come before then."

Sara replied, "Listen, no kid of mine is going around looking like a plucked chicken! Mike has plenty of money. He isn't counting on that check."

We lugged the big packages outside and put them in the back of the jeep. Then Sara had another great idea. "If we eat burgers and fries, we can get home in plenty of time for fishing."

All the way home I hung onto my seat with one hand, and my new boots with the other. I kept remembering what Sara said in the store. *"No kid of mine* is going around looking like a plucked chicken." I wondered if she meant it when she said "no kid of mine." Maybe I was doing things right, for a change. Maybe she was liking me already! Most foster parents take kids so they can get that child-care check. I felt real good that Sara and Mike took me *before* they got any money.

The next morning, and the next, and many days after, I had breakfast with Mike. He taught me to cook bacon, and flip hotcakes. It's not easy. He talked to me, too. I never had a man talk to me about fishing and logging and trucks. For all this, the only thing I had to do was look after Sara. Every single morning he made me promise to do that. He would say, "I am counting on you, Joey. Take care of Sara for me. Don't let her get hurt. Okay?"

"Promise," I always answered. I still didn't know what he meant, and was afraid to ask. I didn't want him to think I was a dummy. I watched him, so maybe I could learn something. I am good at watching people. I can see lots. Mike was sure good to Sara. She was good to him. Both were so good to me I couldn't believe it. Not gushy good. Everyday good. No big production. Secretly I kept wondering when things would start to go bad, like they always did before.

To keep things going good, I made my bed and helped with the chores. After Mike trained me, I took on a really big job. He called it a "responsibility." It was up to me to put gas in the jeep, check the oil, and be sure we had fresh drinking water in the jug before we went fishing. Mike did not want us to get stranded in the mountains. Boy, was I careful! I didn't want to get stranded, and have to stay out overnight in the dark woods.

I did something else, too. Even though I am scared to death of bears and snakes, I watched for them when we were fishing. Like Mike, I didn't want Sara to get hurt. Or me either. Besides, he had told me this secret. He said that even though Sara was a big woman, she needed a man to look after her. When he was gone to work, I was that man.

I snorted. "Who are you kidding, Mike?"

He waggled a finger under my nose. "I'm telling you the same thing I told our two boys when they were your age. They were to look after their mother when I was not around. Sara is your mother now. Got the message?"

I got the w-h-o-l-e message.

Maybe you got the message, too. I guess now you know why I never once ran away the first month I lived with Sara and Mike. Or the second month. They didn't know it, but that was a record for me.

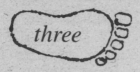

three

I KNOW I haven't said a word about Bigfoot yet. Keep your shirt on. I am coming to that pretty quick now.

Remember how Sara said all I had to do was fish and hike with her? At first we fished a creek not too far from the cabin. Bingo always went with us. I learned to set up my own rod and reel, and load the hook with worms or grasshoppers. And I caught fish! They were small trout. The yucky part was having to clean out their insides so Sara could cook them. She said, "Every fisherman has to clean his own catch." No kidding, trout taste a lot different than the fish sticks served on the school lunch.

All this time I was afraid of the woods, but didn't let on. Well, the first day I hinted a little. At lunch time we sat on a log. I said, "Gee, it's so quiet it's spooky."

Sara shook her head. "You got cotton in your ears? Listen. You'll hear lots of good things."

Little by little I got used to forest noises. Then one day there was this big crash. I almost chewed my heart. Sara explained it was caused by a dead branch falling to the ground. She showed me the branch. It was bigger around than I am! No wonder it made a lot of noise. I laughed so she wouldn't think I was scared. "A bear wouldn't make that big a noise, would it?"

Sara told me two things. Bears don't fall out of trees. And, during summer bears stay up in the high country, way up the mountainside.

I was awfully glad to learn that. "What about mountain lions?"

"They were all shot dead long ago."

"Oh. What about snakes?"

"Rattlesnakes? Naw. They like dry ground and sun-warmed rocks. These woods are too cool and damp."

"Boy, you sure know a lot about the woods."

Sara grunted. "Some folks don't think so." When I asked "What folks?" she changed the subject.

I was glad she knew so much, and said so. But it puzzled me. I still hadn't figured out why Mike kept telling me to look after Sara. If I didn't have to watch out for bears or snakes, what was I supposed to be doing?

I have got to say this. Another thing that helped me get used to the woods was Bingo. That cat really loved the woods. He'd take off hunting, alone, and not show up until I called him. The weird thing was, he always knew when we were going to town for groceries. He would disappear. Sara said he was scared to death of being in town. Once he got taken there by mistake. He growled and slunk under the seats, and would not leave the jeep. Isn't that something? Here I was, a city kid scared of the woods. Here he was, a country cat scared of the city. Only I was getting less scared of the woods every day.

Now, because of what happened pretty soon after that, I better describe the country a little. In southwestern Washington, there are miles and miles and miles of forests. There are also mountain peaks sticking up in every direction. Some are famous, like Mount Rainier. It is 14,410 feet high. Another one is Mount St. Helens. It is only 9,671 feet high. It looks like the biggest vanilla ice cream cone in the world. Sara and I fished the rivers and creeks between these two mountains. We fished the Lewis River, the Cowlitz River, the Toutle River, and some little creeks. If you look at the map in your geography book, you can find right where we fished.

One day when we fished the Lewis River, something strange happened. We waded out from the bank into shallow water. We cast our hooks out to the deep water. We both caught several trout. Then I got a whiff of skunk odor. The smell got stronger and stronger. I called to Sara, "P-ugh! Skunks!"

Sara wears an old canvas hat with her fishing lures stuck in the band. She pushed back her hat, and sniffed. She reminded me of a deer sniffing something that could mean danger. "Reel in! Fast!" she called to me. She reeled in her line and eased out of the water onto the bank. When I splashed after her, she hissed, "Quiet!"

I followed her into a thicket of deer brush. We stood together, her arms around me.

"Don't move," she warned.

I didn't. It wasn't easy because flies were biting.

That smell got even worse! It smelled like a hundred skunks. Then we heard sounds like maybe an elephant was tromping through the forest. Even I know there aren't any elephants roaming about the Washington woods.

I was pretty sure a bear was making those noises. It had to be a b-i-g bear. I held my breath. I mean, I was scared! That heavy-footed creature passed within a stone's throw of us . . . clump, thump, clump, thump. We didn't see it. I guess it didn't see us. Whew! Pretty soon the noise and the smell went away.

Sara relaxed and stepped out into the open. "That was close, wasn't it?"

I looked her square in the eye. "Was it a bear?"

Sara rolled her eyes. "Did you see a bear? I didn't." She checked her wristwatch. "It's time to go, Joey. Let's head back to the jeep."

I followed right behind her. "If that wasn't a bear, what was it?"

Sara turned and faced me. "Forget it! Okay?"

It wasn't okay. I said so. Besides, I had this creepy feeling. I imagined there was maybe a wild beast hiding somewhere, waiting to pounce on us.

"No, no," Sara replied. "Trust me. There is nothing to be afraid of."

"Then why did you stop fishing and hide in the bushes?"

"Not because I was afraid."

32

I still wasn't satisfied. I stomped my feet. "You're keeping a secret! That's not fair."

If Sara heard me, she did not let on. She walked to the jeep. For two cents I would have thrown a tantrum. I would have yelled and kicked my heels until she told me her secret. But I didn't. The deep woods is no place for a tantrum. Whatever made those thumping noises might hear me, and come back! Then I remembered I could ask Mike for answers.

When we got back to the jeep, Bingo was nowhere in sight. The minute Sara started the engine, he streaked out of the woods. As usual, he leaped up onto my lap.

Sara pointed her thumb at Bingo. "See, he's not afraid. If there was a dangerous wild animal around, he'd let us know."

I still pouted, even though Sara probably was right. I stayed mad all the way home, and until bedtime. The next morning I told Mike what happened. "What do you think made those thumpy noises?"

All he said was, "How would I know? I wasn't there."

I glared at him. "Aw, Mike, come on. Does Sara know?"

"She might."

"Well, heck, why didn't she tell me? What's the big secret?"

"Sara will tell you when she's ready."

My eyes nearly popped out of my head. "Then there *is* something weird out there in the forest!"

Mike laid a hand on my shoulder. "If you're smart, Joey, you won't pester Sara for an answer right now."

By this time I would not let anything happen so that Sara or Mike would hand me back to Mrs. Adams. I never had it so good. I really worked hard to keep things good. But I still didn't know for sure if they liked me. It takes a foster kid a long time to be sure about things like that. Making people like you is real hard. You sure can get fooled. I know! So, I swallowed the questions I still wanted to ask. I didn't want Sara or Mike mad at me.

Sara and I fished many days in different places. She tried to teach me the names of different trees and animals and birds. Now I could care less about things like that, and said so. Oh, did Sara get mad at me! She bellowed, "You listen when I tell you something. Do you want to be a dumb kid all your life?"

After that I paid attention.

I got so I liked sitting quietly on a log in the forest, and listening. It's shady and cool. The trees are so tall their branches blot out the sunlight. Here and there, though, sunbeams light up the forest floor. It is almost never quiet. You can hear birds any time. I love to hear a woodpecker pecking away, or a jay squawking, or the *wook-to-wook* call of quail. When the wind blows gently, it whistles and wails through the branches.

Sara told me the Indians thought those noises were the voices of spirits. She said they were not. They were caused by the wind.

If you sit quietly, and don't talk, you can see chipmunks and squirrels scamper up and down tree trunks. Grouse fly right over your head. Sometimes deer appear, and stare at you. Birds chirp back if you whistle at them.

Now and then, you see things that are strange.

One day Sara and I hiked way high in the mountains. When we rested on a fallen tree trunk, I spied something. Ahead was an old Douglas fir tree. I bet it was eight feet across, and nearly two hundred feet tall. It had a huge slab of bark partly pulled off the trunk. "Hey, Sara, did lightning peel off that bark?"

We walked closer. The bark of an old Douglas

fir tree is very rough. It can be two to three inches thick. It is dark, and crisscrossed with deep furrows. You can't pick it loose with your fingernails, or a pocket knife. But here we were, looking at a loose slab as large as a kitchen door. Even I could tell lightning had not hit the tree.

I asked, "Did a bear do that?"

Sara shook her head. There were no scratches to show if a bear had clawed the bark loose. But something did it, something as strong as a bear. Sara braced one foot against the lower part. She tugged hard on the loose piece and still could not budge it. We picked at the soft spongy fibers between the bark and the wood. They were almost covered with grubs, which are wormlike insect eggs.

By now Sara had taught me to know the different tracks made by deer, raccoon, badger, chipmunks, and quail. So, I got down on my hands and knees, and looked for tattletale tracks. I saw clumps of wild ferns mashed down, and a broken wild azalea bush. Then I let out a yelp. "Sara! Look-y here!"

She bent over to look close. "How about that? A footprint!"

"It's a whopper! Look, here's more! Here's one for the left foot, and another for the right foot." I stood up and pressed my right foot on one. Mine was only half as big, and I was wearing boots. My voice got all squeaky. "Sara! This footprint is more than twice as long as mine! It's bigger than yours. Who's been walking barefooted around here? If you know, you've got to tell me."

That Sara! She made me so mad. Do you know what she was doing? Smiling!

"It's not funny," I yelled at her. "Where did those footprints come from?"

Sara thought for a long time. Then she said, "Well, I guess I better tell you. I think Bigfoot made those tracks."

"Bigfoot! The monster?"

I remembered a television program and a movie I had seen about this Bigfoot monster. It was supposed to be seven or eight feet tall, hairy all over, and walked upright like a man. It made barefoot prints like a man does, only twenty or more inches long and seven inches wide. That's big!

When Sara said Bigfoot's name, I looked in six directions all at once. My heart thudded in my chest. I shivered all over. "I'm gettin' out of here!"

Sara caught me before I ran. "Joey, listen to me. Stop shaking. Don't be afraid. Trust me. There is no reason to be afraid."

."B-b-but Bigfoot could be hiding behind one of these trees!"

"No, he's not."

"Oh, yeah? Well, how can you tell?"

"Remember the day you smelled that bad odor, and we hid in the brush? Bigfoot made that big stink. You don't smell it now, do you? If Bigfoot was close by, you would."

I gulped. "That was—that smell—and those thumpy noises! That was Bigfoot? We were that close to a Bigfoot monster?"

Sara nodded. "I think so. But you do not have to believe me."

"Why not? I believe you."

Sara hugged me. "Oh, Joey, thanks for saying that! Lots of folks think I am crazy. Look, let's sit down and talk about Bigfoot. Okay?"

I was busting to talk about Bigfoot, but not here. I said that.

"All right, we'll go home. No talking until then. Fair enough?"

"Fair enough."

We hurried back to the jeep, put ourselves and Bingo inside, and raised dust all the way back to the cabin.

38

four

IT IS A LOT easier to talk about a big-footed monster when you're safe at home. Sara and I sat on the
davenport. Bingo crawled up on my lap.

Sara began, "First, tell me what you know about
Bigfoot."

What I knew was what most kids know from
watching movies or television. Both showed pictures of a hairy wild monster with long arms, almost no neck, and a pointed head. The face re-
minds you of a gorilla. Or ape. I don't know the
difference. In the movie the monster was walking
upright like a man. It was striding across a sunny
meadow, and then disappeared into the forest. The
pictures were exciting! Imagine, a real *live* monster! However, the man telling the story about the

pictures said most folks thought they were a hoax. They said the monster was only a tall man wearing a gorilla costume.

"What do you think?" Sara asked. "Do you believe there is such a monster?"

I shivered. "After today I sure do. Don't you?"

Sara took a deep breath. Then she said, "Joey, I *know* there is a Bigfoot monster. I have seen one."

"Where?"

Sara saw the monster near where we saw the footprints. She was sitting on a log, resting. Then she began to smell a skunk. At least, she thought it was a skunk. Next she heard thumpy footsteps. Not long after, a Bigfoot appeared on the trail. It was only thirty feet from her! It stopped. It just stood there, and stared and stared at her.

"I never moved. But I looked it over from head to toe. Joey, this creature was nearly eight feet tall. It was a full-grown male. The hair was black, and two or three inches long. The hair covered everything but its face, and fingernails and toenails. It had small ears, hardly any neck, and reddish squinty eyes.

"You won't believe this . . . Studying that monster was so exciting, I forgot to be scared. The monster never made a sound. It never raised a hand, or moved toward me. Suddenly it turned around and walked out of sight. The noise it made as it stepped on dry sticks and fallen logs faded out. After a while, even the smell was gone."

I whistled. "Wow, wow, wow! Then what did you do?"

Sara said she ran lickety-split to the jeep and raced home. Mike wasn't there, so she telephoned her friends in town. Only, they made fun of her. One asked her if she was drunk! Another called the newspaper and television station in Seattle. Reporters and cameramen came to the cabin the next morning. "I didn't want my picture taken, Joey. I don't wear fancy clothes. I don't have my hair frizzed at the beauty parlor. I'm just a country woman. And I'm homely. I know that. But I am not crazy in the head, or a liar."

"Mike believed you, I bet."

"Mike, and the children. I told them all they didn't have to believe me, but they did."

Sara continued her story. After people saw her on television, they called the cabin day and night. Most wanted her to guide them to see the monster so they could kill it, and make a lot of money. She refused, even when they offered to pay her. Others called to say she was crazy, and ought to be locked up. One man said Bigfoot came out of the woods because she looked like his girlfriend. Then he laughed, and hung up. Sara was so hurt she cried.

That afternoon, a Sunday, crowds drove out to the cabin. They demanded to know where Bigfoot was. They walked anywhere they pleased. Some tried to steal the chickens, and helped themselves to vegetables from the garden. Mike called his logger friends for help. They came right away, and ran the strangers off the property.

I just had to interrupt. "Did your logger friends believe you had seen the monster?"

Most did, because they had seen it, too. In the late summer when huckleberries ripened on the mountain, they would see the monster sometimes. They never talked about it because they did not want strangers poking fun at them. Even the loggers who never saw the monster believed Sara. They knew she would never tell whopping lies.

Sara told me something sad. What hurt her most was that all this made a lot of trouble for her kids. "Jim and Al got in fistfights at school. Their pals said I was a nut. Mary and Lisa had the same problem. They did some hair-pulling and scratching. All four kids nearly got kicked out of school.

Mike had to hire a lawyer to get everything calmed down. So, ever since then . . . that happened four years ago . . . I never breathe a word about Bigfoot to anyone. Except Mike."

"And me," I reminded her. "Now tell me more about Bigfoot."

Sara replied, "The trouble is, Joey, that no one knows much about the monster. There are very few photographs of it, and most of those are fakes. The creature has never been captured. Many, many hunters hunt for it. So far, no one has killed one. Oh, there is one man who claims he killed one. He froze the body in a cake of ice, and shows it at carnivals and supermarket parking lots. People have to pay to see it. But reporters found out the body in the ice is really a dummy. So it is a fake.

"Mostly, Bigfoot has been seen crouched beside a road. Or striding across a road. Or feeding on berries and leaves, or eating fish. That movie you saw showed a monster walking across a meadow in the mountains."

"Is that meadow near here?" I asked nervously.

It was far away, thank goodness! It was in northern California.

"If we went there, would we see it?"

"Probably not." After the movie was shown,

thousands drove to northern California. They found they had to drive far into the mountains. Then they had to leave their cars, and hike or ride horseback miles and miles. None of them saw the monster, or his footprints. The footprints have washed away in the rain.

"Was Bigfoot hiding from these people?"

Sara thought Bigfoot had moved on to another place. It probably wanted to get away from hunters. Also, a creature that huge roams a hundred miles or more in search of food.

That made sense. At school I learned that cattle, and horses, and deer need acres and acres of grass and other plants. Buffalo did, too, in the old days before white men came to our land.

Something really bothered me. How could this Bigfoot have its picture taken in California, and make footprints in Washington, where Sara and I saw them?

Sara was surprised. "Oh, my, I thought you knew! There isn't just one Bigfoot creature. There are hundreds! Maybe over a thousand. There has to be, Joey, in order for the monsters to survive so long. The Indians have known about them for a long, long time. White men exploring the West saw them nearly two hundred years ago! They have been seen in western Canada, and down through Washington, Oregon, and California. There are even reports the monster has been sighted in Minnesota, and Tennessee, and Arkansas, and Florida!"

I don't know much about geography. I don't know where those other states are. But I got the idea, all right. Bigfoot is almost everywhere!

Next I wanted to know if anyone had ever seen a baby Bigfoot, or a teenaged Bigfoot, or a mama Bigfoot. The answer was "Yes." But not very often. But there had to be families, or the monster wouldn't survive. I've read about animal families in schoolbooks. There has to be families.

"Sara, there's another name for Bigfoot. I can't remember it. Do you know it?"

Sara knew several names. One popular one was Sasquatch.

"That's it! Sasquatch!"

She told me about that name. Sasquatch is the white man's way of saying an Indian word, *soss q'atl.* It is spelled other ways, too. It means "wild man of the woods." People in British Columbia in Canada, and in our state of Washington call the monster Sasquatch. People in Oregon and California call it Bigfoot. But Sasquatch and Bigfoot are the same. There are other names, Indian names which I can't say or spell. Sara said that down in Florida, the creature is called a Skunk Ape. That makes sense. Folks down there say the ones they saw smelled like a skunk, and looked like an ape!

Of course, I had to know the answer to my next question. Otherwise, I would never walk in the woods again.

I asked, "Is Bigfoot dangerous?"

Sara did not lie. "It could be. We know how other wild animals act if they are bothered. They can be dangerous. But we know this, too. The monster is very, very shy. It keeps out of sight as much as possible. Still, people have found footprints around campgrounds, or trucks and road-building machinery parked on mountain roads. There is no record of a Bigfoot tearing up a campsite, the way bears do. I know of only one story about the monsters attacking people. As I said before, Bigfoot is very shy. It may spy on you, but it will stay away from you. I been searching for it ever since I first saw it. But I haven't found it."

Well, I just had to hear the story about the monsters attacking people. Here is the way Sara told it.

In 1924 some miners were looking for gold in

southern Washington. Gold had been found there long before, but not in big amounts like in California. These men poked around the canyons on the east and north slopes of Mount St. Helens. Remember, that's the mountain I said looked like a big vanilla ice cream cone. Anyway, the men found a small vein of gold in rocks halfway up a steep canyon. They built a small cabin up there for eating and sleeping, and storing their tools. One day the miner named Fred Beck took his rifle and went hunting. He and his friends were out of meat. They had plenty of beans and coffee, but no meat. Mr. Beck climbed to the top rim of the canyon. There he got an awful scare.

Fred Beck spied an enormous apelike monster, and shot it. It was not a bear. It was seven or eight feet tall, hairy all over, but walked upright like a man. He knew bears don't do that. They can stand up on their hind feet, and maybe take a few steps, but they don't walk like a man. They get down on all fours. This creature's face reminded him of an ape, so he shot it. The thing screamed and toppled backward over the rim, or cliff. Its body landed far, far below in a foaming creek. When Fred Beck and his friends climbed down there, the carcass had washed away.

That night all the miners had a terrible scare. They wakened when heavy rocks crashed down on their cabin roof. Angry screeching creatures tried to tear the walls apart. The miners poked holes between the logs, and shot at the attackers. They couldn't see them because it was dark. Hours passed before the shrieking stopped. Then the attackers slunk away in the dark.

At daylight the miners crept outside. All they saw were a few huge barefoot tracks. Some of the rocks thrown down on the rim were too heavy for even two men to lift. All felt that "apes" like the one Fred Beck killed had attacked them, and would come back. So the miners fled. They never ever went back for their belongings. Ever after that place was called Ape Canyon.

"Where is that Ape Canyon?" I had to know.

After Sara told me, I wished I hadn't asked. Ape Canyon was only maybe fifty miles from where we saw the footprints. I remembered something. "You said a creature that large would have to roam a hundred miles or more to get enough food. Does that mean it could come this far from Ape Canyon?"

Sara nodded. Then she asked me, "Joey, now that you know this much about the monster, do you want to stay home? Would you rather not hike in the woods with me?"

Wow! What a question! What a picklement I was in. I didn't want Sara or Mike to think I was a scaredy-cat. I don't think they have much use for scaredy-cats. I wanted them to think I was brave. I tried to skip around the question by asking another one. "All this time we've been fishing and hiking, did you know we might see the monster?"

She shrugged. "We could have . . . but we didn't!"

"Did you have me come and live here so, if we saw Bigfoot, you would have a witness? I mean, there would be someone who could say you were not lying, or crazy in the head."

Sara made me stand up, face her, and look her square in the eyes. "Joey, listen carefully. I am going to say this only one time. I did not lie when I said I saw Bigfoot. That's why I did not even try to defend myself when people called me a liar. I did not need a witness then. I do not need one now. Understand?"

"Yes, ma'am."

"Also, Mike and I weren't looking for a witness to live with us. We wanted a wonderful boy, one we could love as much as our own kids. Understand?"

Tears came to my eyes. My chin wobbled. "But you didn't know if I would be wonderful. Mrs. Adams told you nobody else wanted me. Did you take me because you felt sorry for me?"

Sara put her arms around me, and kissed me. "No, no, no! We did not feel sorry for you. In fact, we were glad you didn't belong to anyone who might take you away from us some day. That way, you could belong to us, like our own kids."

A tear ran down my nose and into my mouth. I didn't care. "Then you aren't going to send me back to Mrs. Adams?"

"Not unless you want to move somewhere else. We love you, Joey. We want you to love us."

Well, I blubbered like a baby. I don't care if I was ten years old, and not supposed to cry like a baby. Only this time, I was crying because I was happy. I hugged Sara. She hugged me back, a big bear hug that made my ribs bend.

By the time I quit crying, I knew something else. I knew why Mike always asked me to look after Sara. He loved her. He didn't want anything bad to happen to her. But if she did get into trouble, or hurt, he wanted someone there to help her, or run for help. Another thing, and I know it sounds silly. The way I looked at it, if we did see Bigfoot, we could talk about it to each other. We could share something, and nobody else could butt in.

So that's why I said, "Sara, if you want to keep on looking for Bigfoot, I'll keep you company."

five

THE NEXT MORNING Sara and I hurried back to
that fir tree. The bark was still dangling from its
trunk. There was not one single grub left on it. We
thought we knew who ripped loose the bark, and
why. The monster must like fat, juicy grubs. But
so do bears, and birds. Besides, there were no new
footprints.

On the short hike from the jeep, we had seen lots
of ripe huckleberries. Sara had told me they were
like candy to bears. We were extra careful, but did
not see any bears around. No Bigfoot, either.

"You think we might see Bigfoot here?"

Sara thought we had a mighty good chance.

I did not know if I wanted to hang around there.
I said that.

"Aw, shucks," Sara exclaimed. "I would like to pick enough huckleberries to make some pies. Mike loves huckleberry pie."

So do I! The more I looked at those berries, the more I wanted pie. "All right. I'll stay." Sara always carries a couple plastic pails in the jeep. We got them and filled them with berries. I filled me, too. I bet I ate as many as Bigfoot would. We went home early so Sara could make pies.

We came back other days. The sunny weather continued. Summer was passing, though. In about a week I would have to start school. "And quit searching for Bigfoot," I complained.

"If we don't see it before then," Sara answered, grinning.

Now I hate to say this, but I have to tell the truth. I believed Sara saw Bigfoot. I believed those footprints by the fir tree were made by Bigfoot. But I really, truly did not think I would ever see that creature face to face. I was only pretending we would, to make Sara happy.

The next morning we went a different direction. We drove to the end of Tincup Creek Road. We parked the jeep, and hiked almost to the top of the mountain. There we discovered we had forgotten to bring our sandwiches and water bottle. So back we went to the jeep. Then I discovered I had forgotten to put the bottle in the jeep. Sara said that was all right. A guy can't think of everything when he has Bigfoot on his mind. But you know how hard peanut butter sandwiches are to swallow unless you have something to drink.

Sara remembered there was a little spring somewhere near. We followed a marked Forest Service trail and then turned off onto a faint deer trail. It ended at the spring. We knelt down for a long drink. Then we washed our hands and faces. Oh, that cool water felt so good! Next Sara told me to take off my shirt and wash under my arms. "You smell bad, Joey."

I sniffed myself. "No, I don't." I giggled.

She rolled her eyes and laughed. "Don't blame me for what we smell."

Then we looked at each other. We stopped laughing. There was an odor around. Not strong, but it was there, all right.

"Bigfoot?" I croaked, my voice scratchy.

Sara beckoned me. We tiptoed away from the spring. We squeezed behind some deer brush. We could lean against a tree while we waited.

"Are we far enough away?" I whispered.

"Shhh! Yes. The smell must be about thirty feet

from here. Far enough, if you don't wiggle."

Me, wiggle? Not me!

We watched and watched. The smell did not fade out. I was sure that meant Bigfoot was watching us. You could have scraped the goosepimples off my arms.

I saw it first.

I know I did, because Sara was looking to her left. I was looking straight ahead at a huge elderberry bush. It was loaded with bluish-purple berries. I figured a monster might like those ripe berries. I was right! First I saw some branches shake. A hand reached out, grabbed a bunch of berries, and tore them loose. Then the hand disappeared!

I jabbed Sara with my elbow, and pointed. I didn't dare whisper.

We stared and stared. Pretty soon the branches shook again. A hand and a hairy arm reached for another bunch of berries. But it couldn't reach far enough. Then two hands and two hairy arms parted the branches. Now we could see a dark shiny face, a big mouth full of teeth, and squinty eyes. The face wasn't as big as I expected. It wasn't all that scary looking.

Sara hugged me, and whispered in my ear, "It's a young one!"

I got so excited I forgot to be quiet. I whistled, and then hollered, "Hey, Bigfoot, come on out!"

The face and hands and arms disappeared.

I smiled and waved, and called some more. Sara did not tell me to stop.

Curiosity must have got to that creature. It came out from behind the bush! It walked like I do, only more clumsy. It squatted down on a fallen log, and stared. Sara was right. It was a young one. Bigger than me by a whole lot, but not a giant.

I slipped v-e-r-y slowly out from behind the bush so Bigfoot could see me. I waved some more. I called several times, "Hi, Bigfoot!"

Boy, did we have a stare-down! I don't know how long it would have lasted. Suddenly, from far away, we heard the loudest, shrillest whistle. The young creature jumped up, and whistled an answer.

Sara leaped out from behind the bush. "Run, Joey! On the double! Back to the jeep!"

I didn't argue. Sara had told me what happened if you got too near a bear cub, and its mama was close by. I beat Sara to the jeep. It was downhill all the way. Even so, we were panting when we piled in and slammed the doors. I rolled down my window so Bingo could jump in. Then I cranked it up while Sara took off in one big spurt. She didn't stop until we got home. When we got out of the jeep, we grabbed hands and danced in a circle, yelling, "Yeow! Whoopee! We saw it, we saw it, we saw Bigfoot!"

Sara fixed lemonade, and we sat on the porch steps. "Well! How did you like seeing Bigfoot?"

I rolled my eyes. "Great! Wow!"

"You're certain it wasn't a bear?"

I shook my head. "That was no bear."

"King Kong, maybe?"

I giggled. "A junior King Kong."

We laughed and talked until Mike came home. Sara let me do all the telling.

Mike believed everything I said. "Gosh, I'm sure happy for you two. I'm glad you both saw the creature. But Joey, how come you didn't bring him home with you?"

I nearly fell off the step, laughing. "I didn't have time to invite him. Next time I see him, I will. I promise."

Him . . . I said *him* now, not *it*. From the time I spied that half-pint-sized monster, I thought of it as a *him*. And I nicknamed him Junior.

During supper I asked, "Can I tell the kids at school that I saw a little Bigfoot?"

Mike looked at Sara. After a minute, she nodded. Mike said it was okay—if I didn't mind kids making fun of me, or mind getting into fistfights when they called me a liar.

Sara hoped that would not happen. I would be attending a small country school. Meadowlark School. All the pupils lived in or near the woods. Their fathers were loggers, or truck drivers, or farmers. Probably some of them had seen Bigfoot, but would never admit it. Some folks are very touchy about being made fun of.

"If I talk about Junior at school, will I get you in more trouble?" I asked Sara.

Mike grunted. "Nothing we can't handle. Right, Sara?"

"Right," she agreed.

It was my story. I could do as I pleased.

The next morning we drove as fast as we dared up Tincup Creek Road. We approached the spring step by step. There was just enough odor to tell us either a skunk or Junior was close by. This time we sat on a log and leaned our backs against another one. We had a good view of the area around the spring.

We waited until I couldn't be quiet any longer. I whistled "Yankee Doodle" as loud as I could.

But Junior did not appear. I was so disappointed I almost cried.

Sara laughed. "Maybe Junior's mama won't let him play with a strange kid."

"But I want to see him again! Maybe we should have brought some food. Do you think he might like cold hotcakes? What about a candy bar?"

Sara reminded me I had only one more day to find out. Tomorrow was Tuesday. The day after, I started school.

Tuesday morning Sara made bologna sandwiches for us. I packed goodies for Junior—a ripe banana, leftover hotcakes with syrup on them, and raw hamburger. I peeled the banana, and left bits of everything near the spring and on fallen tree trunks. Again we sat and waited.

If Junior was watching us, he never let us know. Sara and I got a whiff of his smell now and then. I have to say we could have been smelling a passing skunk. But how could we tell? We never saw a skunk, either.

At three o'clock, Sara said we had to go. "You could sit here a year, and not see him."

I hated to go, and said that.

Sara reminded me that most people never saw a Bigfoot. Never. Ever. Even if they lived in the woods. She read somewhere that none of those who hunt to kill the creature ever see him, either. Most folks who did see a him, or a her, rarely saw either a second time. Sara felt very lucky. She said I should be happy.

I wasn't. I had to see that young Bigfoot again. I did not care about seeing the father or mother that close. Just Junior.

Sara didn't say that was a crazy idea. She just said, "Okay, okay. We've got to go now. But on Saturdays, until snow falls, you and I will keep coming back up the mountain."

That did satisfy me, so we went home.

six

SARA DROVE ME to Meadowlark School the first day. She had to enroll me. I was assigned to Mr. Nelson's room. He taught grades three and four in one room. I have missed so much school I am a third grader.

Mr. Nelson was all right. He invited Sara to stay for the opening exercises. Then he pointed to a blue truck parked in the schoolyard. It had the call letters of a television station painted on the doors. Two men were sitting in it. Mr. Nelson said they were going to film the school buses arriving, and the opening exercises, and classes. Every year the television station did this for their news program. They filmed at one country school and one city school. This year it was Meadowlark School's turn.

I asked if Sara and I could go outside and watch those men. Mr. Nelson said yes. I was very excited about being on television.

Minutes later one school bus came in, and unloaded. The television station cameraman grabbed his camera and took pictures. After the second bus unloaded, I got in line with the kids. We jumped up and down, and waved for the cameraman. Then we marched into the assembly room. It was also an indoor play area and the lunchroom. Before I sat on the floor, I waved at Sara. She was standing in the back. Some lady introduced herself and the teachers. She explained about the television men. After we pledged allegiance to the flag and sang a song, we marched to our classrooms.

Mr. Nelson told each kid where to sit. Third graders sit on one side, fourth graders on the other. My seat was close to the front because I am short. Next the teacher said, "One by one, I want you to stand. Face the class. Speak your name clearly. Tell us what you did this summer."

When my turn came, I said, "My name is Joey Wilson. This summer I saw a real live Bigfoot monster."

Some girls snickered. One boy guffawed loudly,

"Haw, haw, haw." The whole class joined in. Being laughed at made me angry. I felt like sticking out my tongue at everyone. But I didn't. I didn't want to get into trouble my very first day in a new school. So I just stood there.

Mr. Nelson made everyone quiet down. "Joey, is this true? Did you really see a Bigfoot?"

I nodded and crossed my heart. "Honest."

Those darn kids whooped and laughed again. Someone hollered, "Liar!"

No one calls me liar without getting punched in the nose. I said this.

Mr. Nelson called for quiet. "Joey, please describe what you saw. Briefly."

So I did. Briefly.

The kids listened. After I finished, Mr. Nelson asked if any of them had ever seen a Bigfoot. No one raised a hand, or said anything.

"Class, I have an idea. It might be interesting to start the year with a Nature Study project on Bigfoot. Now, you do not have to believe there is a creature like Bigfoot. We can learn a great deal about the forests and mountains of Washington. We can study about the trees, shrubs, animals, and birds. Then we will find out how people use the forests."

One rude kid shouted, "I'd rather study about Bigfoot."

The pupils also shouted, "Yes, yes, let's study about Bigfoot." They clapped and stomped. Mr. Nelson had a hard time making them be quiet.

I said, "If you want me to, I can show you where I saw Bigfoot."

Again the kids were noisy. "Let's have a field trip to see Bigfoot!"

On the side wall was a large map of the state of Washington. Mr. Nelson took his pointer and showed us where the Meadowlark School was on the map. Then he asked me to point to where I had seen Bigfoot. "How did you get there?"

I explained you drove up to the end of Tincup Creek Road. You parked, walked along a Forest Service trail a short way. Then you followed the game trail to the spring. "Bigfoot was at the spring."

Before I could say more, the cameraman and reporter came into the room. The reporter told us just to relax and look natural. "Don't make any faces. And Mr. Nelson, keep your pointer on the map. You—" he meant me, and wrote down my name, "you stand right where you are, facing the teacher. Continue the lesson, Mr. Nelson."

The cameraman had a big camera strapped on his left shoulder. That camera was as big as a calf, and as awkward. When the reporter told him to start filming, he did. The reporter had a microphone in his hand. When Mr. Nelson or I spoke, he pointed it in our direction.

Mr. Nelson said, "Class, shall we continue discussing plans for our field trip into the mountains? Joey, tell us again how to reach the spring you described earlier."

I repeated the directions.

The reporter butted in. "Mr. Nelson, will you tell the television viewers the purpose of this field trip? What value has this trip to the pupils' studies?"

Our teacher explained, "This will be a Nature Study field trip. Pupils learn more about the forest and its animals, birds, and trees when they see them firsthand. They should see many birds, possibly a golden eagle, and squirrels, deer . . . and other creatures. Joey told us he had seen a Bigfoot monster this summer. I believe the other popular name for the creature is Sasquatch. The pupils will take notes about the creature's habitat. They will decide for themselves if Bigfoot is real."

The reporter said, "Thank you, Mr. Nelson.

And now, viewers, our roving camera will move to the next room."

As the cameraman backed out of our room, the reporter asked Mr. Nelson, "When is the class field trip? If you really are going to search for Bigfoot, I would like to do a special film report on it."

The field trip would have to be soon, in two or three weeks while the weather was still good. Mr. Nelson said he would let the reporter know the exact day.

"One more thing," the reporter added. "I was very interested in learning that that boy, Joey, saw Bigfoot. After we finish filming in the next room, could we interview Joey on camera? Viewers enjoy knowing when and where Bigfoot is sighted."

"You would need the mother's permission, I am sure. She was here earlier." Mr. Nelson looked out the window. "Yes, there she is. Joey, you may be excused to talk to your mother. You may stay outside until the reporter is ready to film your story."

I strutted out of the room and down the hall and across the playground. Sara had stayed to talk to the woman who cooks the hot lunches. They were long-time friends. I asked Sara if I could tell my story on television. "I know I can, but I wanted you to know."

Sara nodded. "It's your story."

I told her about the field trip. "Mr. Nelson needs mother helpers that day. Will you mother-help?"

"You bet."

Very soon the television men came outside. Sara told them they were not to ask me where we lived, or exactly where we saw Bigfoot. This was for our protection, and Bigfoot's. She did not want strangers bothering us all day and night, or hunting that little creature with guns. The men were nice. They understood. But they did ask Sara to be in the picture.

She refused. "No, sir! You leave me out. This is Joey's story."

I had to stand with one hand pointing toward the mountains. The reporter asked me these questions:

"Joey, when did you see Bigfoot?"

"What did it look like?"

"Did it do anything to frighten you?"

"Would you like to see Bigfoot again?"

If you saw me on television, you already know the answers I gave. There is no use telling the same story twice.

The reporter finished by saying, "Thank you, Joey, for bringing us such exciting news about your Bigfoot sighting. If you ever see the creature again, be sure and let us know."

I promised. I also thanked him for letting me tell my story on television.

Remember that?

Maybe you didn't see me on television. Did you read about me in the Seattle newspaper? Or in *The Weekly Reader?*

I bet you thought that was the whole story, didn't you?

It wasn't. Keep reading. There's lots more to tell.

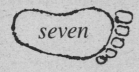

seven

AFTER THE TELEVISION crew drove away, Sara walked with me to the school door.

"Gosh, Sara, I didn't have time to tell half the story," I complained.

"You were wonderful. Wait until Mike knows you are going to be on television tonight. He will be so proud. So will I! We will all watch the program together. Maybe I should make a chocolate cake to celebrate."

I asked her not to frost the cake until I got home. I wanted to lick the bowl. She promised. I went back into the schoolroom.

During morning recess some boys in my class razzed me about Bigfoot. One boy named Ben called me a liar right to my face.

Even if he was a fourth grader, I shook my fist under his nose. "You want to say that again?"

Ben backed off. "Sorehead! Can't you take a joke?"

During lunch and on the school bus going home, I got called other names. Almost everybody was making fun of me. I don't know who did it, but somebody called me "Bigfoot" Wilson.

This Ben character hollered, "Naw, naw! You mean Bigmouth Wilson, tellin' all that junk about a monster."

It is against the rule to stand up when the bus is in motion. I stood up anyway, and shoved my face right at Ben's. "Oh, yeah? Well, who do you have to thank for the field trip?"

Other kids pulled me back on my seat. They told Ben to shut up. "Joey's right. We get to have a fun trip on account of him."

We got pretty noisy. Mrs. Welby, the driver, stopped the bus. She informed us she would not move until everyone acted like a lady or a gentleman. We settled down.

When I walked in the house, Sara exclaimed, "Joey, you look hoppin' mad. What happened?"

I told her. "Those kids are just jealous because I got to talk twice on television."

It was not nice of them, Sara admitted. "Now you know how I felt when people said bad things to me. But Joey, tell the truth. Haven't you made fun of boys and girls when you went to other schools?"

Well, I had. Who hasn't? I have called kids Fatso, Pegleg, Dirty Face, Dumbo, Slant-eyes. All kids do that.

Sara told me to grin, and forget it. Next week the kids would be calling someone else names.

My chin stuck out like a shovel. "Boy, I'd sure like to whack back at them."

"Forget it!" Sara bellowed. "One more word like that and you can't frost the cake."

I frosted the cake, and licked the bowl clean.

That night, when it was time for the "Evening News Roundup," Mike and Sara and I sat on the davenport to watch. I was great. I really was! I didn't know I could be so good.

After the film about me was over, we all groaned. It was over so fast! I could have cried. There was much more I could have told. We wanted to hear my story again. But you know how television is. Flash! you're on! Flash! you're off!

Mike said parts of the newscast might be shown again on the "Ten O'clock News Roundup." I could stay up late and watch it.

I stayed up for another reason: so I could have another piece of cake.

When Mike tucked me in bed, he said, "Something is bothering you, Joey. Want to tell me about it?"

I told him. Then I said, "I'm not mad anymore. I was, but not now. I don't want to do anything mean. But I sure want to play a joke on the kids in my room who called me names."

Mike sat on the edge of the bunk. "Got any ideas?"

I sure had. I told him. It was a swell idea, if I do say so.

Mike called Sara into the bedroom. I told her my idea. "Will you help me?"

Sara said she would, providing I told the teacher.

"Aw, no! That would spoil the fun!"

Sara would not budge. Either I told the teacher, and he approved, or the joke was off.

Mike agreed. "Sara is right, Joey. Mr. Nelson has to approve."

"Oh, okay." They kissed me good night and turned out the light. I guess guys in the third grade are too old to be kissed like that. Maybe so for kids

72

who are used to it. I wasn't, and I liked it. I went right to sleep so morning would come faster.

Mr. Nelson listened carefully when I talked to him at recess. He thanked me for letting him in on the secret. It would be all right to pull my joke. Later he told the class he had talked to the principal about the field trip. It would take place in two weeks, on a Friday, if it wasn't raining.

All day in class we studied for the field trip. We also planned the field trip. The thing we argued most about was the food. Not for Bigfoot. For us. We agreed on Monsterburgers, buns, potato chips, catsup and mustard, Kool-Aid and cupcakes. We invited four grown-ups to mother-help. Sara was one.

I was voted Leader.

After lunch Mr. Nelson read to us about Bigfoot. He had checked out a book from the school library. Its title was *On the Track of Bigfoot*. He read the chapter about the man who took that famous photograph of a Bigfoot. All of us had seen that picture on television, or in newspapers, or *The Weekly Reader*. You know the one . . . it shows a hairy apelike monster striding across a meadow in the mountains in northern California.

Mr. Nelson told us, "Roger Patterson is the man

who took that picture. He searched seven years ... yes, seven long years before he saw the creature. So, don't you be disappointed if you don't see Bigfoot on the field trip."

This book had pictures of Roger Patterson and his famous monster film. It also showed plaster casts made from a Bigfoot's footprint. They were huge! There were also pictures of people who have seen Bigfoot, or hunt the monster. Mr. Nelson turned the pages slowly so we could see the pictures. They were exciting.

Everyone in class wanted to read the book. Mr. Nelson said he would read one chapter each day. Other times, the book would be on the classroom library shelf. It had to be returned to the school library in two weeks.

A girl named Suzie raised her hand. "My mother says there is no such thing as a Bigfoot."

"There might not be," the teacher answered. "No one can prove if there really is a monster like that, or not. But remember, Roger Patterson claimed he filmed a real monster. Joey Wilson claims he saw one only last week. Both have a right to say they saw the monster. In America, people can say and believe what they want. Can't they? We have freedom of speech and thought, don't we?

Until someone captures a Bigfoot, or finds a dead one, we will not know for sure, will we?

"Let me give you an example. You all know what a gorilla is, and looks like, don't you?"

Hands went up all over the room.

"Well, long ago, in South Africa, native hunters told white men stories about a giant-sized 'wild man' that lived deep in the jungle. They said this creature was much larger than a chimpanzee, and very, very shy. Even the best hunters rarely saw it. When scientists in Europe and America were told about it, they scoffed. They said no wild man or ape that huge could possibly exist. But then a young man named Paul du Chaillu traveled deep into the jungle. He stayed there with native helpers until he shot one. He brought the carcass back to the United States. After scientists examined it, they admitted it was a giant ape. They called it the gorilla."

Mr. Nelson knew another example. He told us, "Years later, some time after 1900, there were stories in the newspapers and magazines about a giant-sized, black-and-white bear in China. Again, scientists said flatly there could be no such creature. Time after time, expert hunters and even zoo people went to China to capture one. Time after time, they came back empty-handed. Then suddenly, several of these creatures were captured, and studied. Scientists learned they were not bears, but members of the raccoon family." Mr. Nelson smiled. "Class, what animal was that?"

"The giant panda," most everybody hollered.

"Correct. Now all the world knows about giant pandas. So, who knows? Maybe this will happen with Bigfoot. Maybe some day the mystery about Bigfoot will be solved. Would you like that?"

We all clapped loudly.

For the next two weeks we studied wildlife habitat. Habitat means the place where wild animals live. We studied only the mountain and big tree country near our school. We talked about what wild animals lived there, what they ate, where they slept, and how they raised their young. We also talked about the things which endanger wild animals in our state of Washington. We listed those things on the blackboard this way:

    forest fires
    drought (dried-up springs and creeks)
    pesticide sprays
    deep snow and cold
    logging
    hunters

One boy in class said, "Mr. Nelson, I watch *Wild Kingdom* a lot on television. Why can't someone shoot Bigfoot with a dart with medicine in it, so Bigfoot would go to sleep. That way it could be tied up and put in a cage. Or, it could be measured, and its heartbeat listened to, and snapshots taken. Then it could be left to wake up on its own, if the men did not want to cage it. But they would still have lots of proof that the monster was real."

I called out, "First you got to find Bigfoot!"

Everybody laughed, even the teacher. "Joey is right. First you have to find the monster. Well, maybe we will find one. Let's hope so!"

The bell rang then. Class was dismissed.

We were all glad. We couldn't wait for Field Trip Day to come.

eight

SARA DROVE ME to school on Field Trip Day. The things I needed for my joke were hidden in the back of the jeep. I had to report to my classroom for roll call.

Mr. Nelson divided the class into four groups. The schedule for the day was this:

9:00 A.M.	Bus leaves
10:00 A.M.	Begin hike
11:00 A.M.	Class session
12–12:30 P.M.	Play period
12:30–1:00 P.M.	Lunch
1:15 P.M.	Hike to Bigfoot Springs; return
2:00 P.M.	Bus departs
3:00 P.M.	Arrive Meadowlark School

I was first in line to lead the class onto the bus. The food and play equipment were stacked in the back. Two of the mother-helpers sat in the rear. After all the pupils were seated, Mr. Nelson got on. We sat on the front seat behind the driver. It was my job to tell the driver, Mrs. Welby, where to go. The television cameraman and reporter followed right behind in their truck. Sara came last in her jeep.

It took us almost an hour to reach the end of Tincup Creek Road. The Forest Service had cleared a place where hikers and hunters could park off the road. Mrs. Welby parked there. Before she opened the door, she told us, "Boys and girls, I will remain by the bus all day. The front door, and the emergency back door, will be open at all times. If you have to run like the dickens to escape Bigfoot, you can jump right on the bus. If I see you running and hollering, I will honk the horn to scare Bigfoot away."

Everybody laughed. Secretly I was glad the bus doors would be open.

We left the bus and divided into our groups. Mr. Nelson handed us work sheets and pencils. There were lists to check of things we saw. At the bottom were questions to answer during the class session later on.

The reporter and cameraman followed us everywhere. At first some kids acted up. They waved and made faces. Mr. Nelson stopped that right away. Pretty soon we forgot about being filmed.

Mr. Nelson and I were co-leaders of Group One. The mother-helpers led Group Two and Group Three. Sara was in charge of Group Four. We had to stay in our groups. We knew what could happen if we wandered off alone.

Maybe I should tell you the most important rule if you ever get lost in the woods. *Sit.* Yes, sit. Stay right where you are. Don't holler until you lose your voice. When folks discover you are lost, they will hunt for you. You will hear them, and can yell, "Here I am!"

Anyway, everything went just dandy. I led the hike along the improved Forest Service trail. "Improved" meant all the dangerous rocks, and overhanging limbs, and exposed tree roots had been removed. Every time I pointed out a different kind of tree, or bird, or animal, everyone marked a work sheet.

Now and then someone would holler, "Hey, I smell Bigfoot!" Or, "Hey, I bet this is a Bigfoot footprint!" They were wrong.

We tasted wild huckleberries. We chewed leaves

from plants Bigfoot might eat. We found grubs under rocks. No one had nerve enough to eat one. We saw a wild beehive and deer tracks, but no deer. We really learned a lot. But we did not find out anything new about Bigfoot. Or hear him. Or smell him. Or see him.

We hiked back to the parking lot. After we drank some Kool-Aid, we sat on the ground. Mr. Nelson called out, "Attention! Everybody quiet. Let us begin answering the first question at the bottom of the work sheet. It is, 'Do you think one or more Bigfoot creatures could live in this forest?' "

Hands went up. Most of us said yes. It was scary to think there might be more than one monster. We knew there had to be, if there really was a Bigfoot creature. Otherwise Bigfoot would be extinct. Extinct means "all gone, forever."

We wondered if Bigfoot and his family hibernated in the winter, like bears. We could not decide. Maybe, when it rained and rained, or the snow was deep, the creatures found shelter in caves.

Another question on the work sheet was: Do you think the creatures store up food for winter?

No one knew, but storing up food seemed like a good idea.

The next question was: Do you think the creatures know how to start a fire?

No one knew that, either.

I raised my hand. "Well, people say Bigfoot is curious. Maybe he has watched enough people build fires and cook food to learn about fire."

Mr. Nelson reminded us that surely Bigfoot knew the danger of fires in the forest. Many animals are afraid of fire.

The more we talked, the more we realized how little anyone knew about the monster's habits. If he was real, he was a mystery.

Finally, Mr. Nelson said, "Now, one last question. How many of you now *know* for certain there really is a Bigfoot?"

My hand was the only one that went up.

"Why don't you know?" the teacher asked the rest of the class.

Answers popped up like popcorn.

"We didn't find any proof this morning."

"We didn't see Bigfoot."

"Bigfoot is a fake."

Mr. Nelson asked, "How many can prove there is no Bigfoot?"

Some hands went halfway up. Those kids said they couldn't prove anything, only their parents said there wasn't any such monster.

We handed in our work sheets. Then Mr. Nelson put on a red baseball cap, and started the ball game. At 12:30 P.M. the game ended because it was lunch time. The Monsterburgers the mothers were frying smelled powerfully good. We joked a lot about whether Bigfoot might smell them cooking, and pay us a visit.

No such luck.

After that good lunch, I had to check some things. I checked to be sure the bus doors were open. I told the cameraman it was shady in the forest. If he used bright lights, he might scare Bigfoot away. He said he would use special film and would not need bright lights. Then I asked Mr. Nelson if everything was okay. He said all the grown-ups knew something funny was going to happen.

I was just sick! "You told them my secret?"

"No. I did not tell them what would happen. I did not mention your name. They will be as surprised as the children."

Lastly I checked with Sara. Everything was ready.

When Mr. Nelson blew the whistle, we formed our groups again. "Class, now we are going to hike on an unimproved trail. Animals made this trail long before men came to this forest. Watch your step. Joey says it is not far to the spring. There will be room for us to stand fairly close around it. The ground might be wet in places. Maybe we will see Bigfoot tracks there. If you see a footprint, do not step on it. All right! Are we ready?"

Wouldn't you know? Those dumb kids shouted, "Yes!"

I waved my arms. I was upset. "Qui-et! You want to scare Bigfoot away? Now, keep close together. When I stop, you stop. Look for Bigfoot behind bushes. Sniff hard for his smell. Listen for his footsteps. But no talking!"

I led the way, with Mr. Nelson right behind me. Each mother-helper walked with her group. Sara's group was last. On the way to the spring I stopped several times. Every one sniffed and listened, and looked hard for Bigfoot. I also stopped by the tall bush where Sara and I were hiding when we first saw the young Bigfoot. Next I showed them where I stood when I waved at the creature. We tiptoed on to the spring and started to form a ring around it. Suddenly I pointed. In some mud by the water were two large barefooted footprints. I covered my mouth to keep from hollering. I pointed.

Mr. Nelson held his finger to his lips so everyone was quiet. Since he was smiling, no one got nervous. Of course, some kids pushed and shoved because they weren't close to the footprints.

I whispered, "Mr. Nelson, can the kids move in a circle?" That way everyone could see the footprints up close.

He nodded. First he motioned for the cameraman to come close and take his pictures. After that, everyone who had brought a camera had a chance.

While this was going on, and the kids had their eyes glued on the teacher or the footprints, I sneaked off. I dodged behind trees and shrubs. No one saw me. I followed the trail leading deeper into the woods. Not far, though. Sara was there. We giggled so we could hardly get the monkey costume out of her backpack. She had slipped away during lunch and left it there. I had wanted a gorilla costume, but none was available in my size. I had to settle for a monkey suit. I slipped it on over my clothes, and zipped it up. Next I pulled on fake plastic flippers shaped like giant footprints. They went on over my boots.

"Be careful you don't stumble," Sara whispered.

"Okay, okay." My teeth were chattering I was so nervous.

The headpiece and face mask were in two pieces. The mask was the ugliest thing I ever saw. It made me shiver. I put the headpiece on first. A rubber band held the mask tight against my face. Sara had to pull it around to get the eye holes where I could see through them, also the nose holes and mouth. "Oh, Joey! The rubber band on the face mask shows. You should have put it on under the headpiece."

I didn't have time to change. I hissed, "The kids will be too excited to notice. Where's the fangs?"

She handed me a set of those plastic monster teeth you wear on Halloween. I slipped them over the mouth opening. "Do the fangs show good?" My voice sounded funny.

Sara grinned. "If Bigfoot sees you, he will be scared to death!" She turned me so I faced the spring. "Good luck, Bigfoot!"

I giggled, and stomped along the trail. Clump . . . thump . . . clump . . . thump. I stopped twice and shook branches on small trees. Then I took out the plastic teeth, stuck two fingers in my mouth, and whistled the loudest I could.

I heard Mr. Nelson say loudly, "Class! What was that sound? Did you hear a whistle? Listen!"

I didn't care if he talked out loud now because

I did not want the real Bigfoot to come too close if he was around. But I waited until I hoped the kids were nervous. Then I whistled again. I picked up a branch and whacked it hard against a tree trunk.

"Is Bigfoot coming?" some girl asked in a squeaky voice.

Mr. Nelson laughed very loud, and very hard. "Ha-ha-ha-ha-ha!" That way, the class would know he was not frightened and they shouldn't be. "Can anyone see anything like Bigfoot looking at us?" He peered this way, and that way, until he faced in my direction. "There he is! I see him! There's Bigfoot!"

That was my cue to jump up and down, and shake more branches, and growl. I also parted some branches so the class saw me. The trouble was, I growled so loud the plastic teeth fell out. When I grabbed for them, I let go of the branches. One whacked me on the head. I forgot and yelled, "O-u-c-h!"

For a second it was awfully, awfully quiet. Then that kid named Ben hollered, "That's not Bigfoot! It's a kid wearing a monkey suit. I bet that's Joey Wilson!"

I thought my great joke was ruined. Fortunately, I am a fast thinker. I decided to play it cool. I swaggered out from behind the bush, and spoke in a monsterish voice, "Howdy, kids! Bigfoot Wilson here!"

The kids and mothers nearly fell in the spring, they laughed so hard. Everybody wanted to shake the monster's hand. The cameraman filmed the whole business. Everybody told me what a great joke I pulled. Mr. Nelson explained, "Joey did not want anyone to be disappointed by not seeing Bigfoot. That's why he planned this joke. Isn't that right, Mr. Bigfoot Wilson?"

It wasn't exactly right, but I was not going to argue. I just laughed behind my monkey face mask.

Mr. Nelson checked his watch. He said it was time to march back to the bus. Everybody got in line. I had to take off those plastic flippers so I could walk right.

All of a sudden we heard something else. A loud high whistle! I mean, really loud and high!

Mr. Nelson called out, "Class, listen! What bird call was that?"

Everybody stood still and was very quiet. We all jumped when we heard some wood crackling. Then we heard the whistle again.

I jerked off my mask. "Mr. Nelson! That's the

same whistle I heard when I saw the young Big-foot! Remember, I said there was this awful loud whistle, and the Bigfoot jumped up and ran off into the woods?"

Mr. Nelson nodded. "Yes, we all remember that, don't we, class? Everybody quiet now. Maybe we will see a real Bigfoot in a moment."

We did! We saw some bushes shake, and then they parted, and there was a huge Bigfoot! All we could see was the head and shoulders.

That kid named Ben yelled, "Run, run! Bigfoot is gonna get us!"

A mother-helper grabbed him as Mr. Nelson shouted, "No, no! Bigfoot will not come near so many of us."

Some of us waved, and the creature growled, shook the bushes, and disappeared. Then Mr. Nelson ordered, "Fall in line! March to the bus! No pushing and shoving." He led the way out of the woods at a fast pace, but not too fast.

The bus driver had the motor running. When she saw Mr. Nelson, she started honking the horn. She kept the door open while he helped everyone board the bus. After he got on, she closed the door, revved the motor, and slowly drove onto the road.

Mr. Nelson sat on the seat where I was. He

shook my hand and whispered, "Joey, the joke was great!"

I was so happy I was shaking. Of course, I agreed with him.

The kids were awfully noisy. After the bus drove around a curve, the teacher asked Mrs. Welby to stop the bus. She did, but kept the lights flashing like it was a regular stop. Mr. Nelson stood, and faced the class. "Quiet now . . . quiet." Then he asked me to stand. "Class, I think we owe Joey a vote of thanks for making it possible for us to end our field trip by seeing Bigfoot. Everybody give him a big hand."

They clapped, and stomped and whistled. I slipped the mask on, and the plastic teeth, and took a bow.

Next Mr. Nelson said, "How did you like seeing that big Bigfoot? Wasn't that great?"

Everybody agreed, except one spoilsport. There's one in every bunch. It was Ben. He said, "Aw, that was a fake Bigfoot, too."

Wow! The kids got in a whale of an argument over whether it was a fake, or not. The teacher finally said, "The cameraman filmed it all. I am sure he will have the answer."

Just then Mrs. Welby interrupted. "Here come

the other two cars, Mr. Nelson."

We all craned our necks to see the cameraman and reporter in their truck, and Sara in her jeep, coming around the curve. "Class, now they have caught up with us, everybody sit back and relax. We have had a very exciting day. Let's be quiet on the drive back to school. You may whisper, but no loud talking."

So we did. I kept the face mask on. I had to. I just could not playact anymore. I didn't want anyone to see the smirky smile on my face.

When the bus stopped in the schoolyard, Mr. Nelson thanked the mother-helpers and the driver for making it such a good day. He said nice things about how we boys and girls behaved. He thanked me again for my joke.

The cameraman and reporter thanked us, too. They said we were wonderful actors. When the kids asked if they thought the big Bigfoot was real or a fake, they said they really didn't know. It would take some time to have the film developed. When it was ready, they would show it to all the pupils of Meadowlark School, their parents and grandparents, and aunts and uncles and cousins, and friends and neighbors. Then everybody would study the film of the big Bigfoot and decide whether it was real or not.

We thanked them, and waved good-bye. Then we all marched off the bus because our parents were waiting for us.

Sara hugged me. I hugged her. She helped me get out of the costume. We would have to drive to town now, and return it to the costume rental store. By the time we got home Mike was already there. He had dinner waiting. We were all starved but it took a long time to eat because we talked and laughed so much.

After dessert Mike said, "Yessir, Joey, that was a super joke you thought up."

Sara added, "Well, sure. Why wouldn't it be super? Joey's a super kid."

That's what I like about Mike and Sara. When they believe something, they say it right out. They don't keep it a secret. That's what counts. Now it was my turn. I said, "Well, you know how it is. If a kid is a super kid, it's because he has a super mom and dad."

They really liked hearing that. So now you know why I never run away from home. Now I have the kind of home you don't run away from.

The next Monday morning Mr. Nelson had us all write reports on the field trip. Then we drew pictures. All the reports and drawings were displayed in the school hallway so all the kids and teachers and visitors could see them.

Meanwhile, though, our class kept arguing whether that big Bigfoot was a bear, or a real Bigfoot, or a fakeroo. That's what Ben said it was—a fakeroo, probably some father in a gorilla suit. "I bet a quarter that was Jocy's dad," he bragged.

"It was not!" I answered. "My dad worked that day." Some of the kids knew this was true because their dads worked with Mike. They said this. I was so happy they backed me up that I did not make Ben pay me that quarter.

Finally, the movie of the class field trip was shown at the school. The assembly room was jam-packed. No one even coughed once during the whole thing. I nearly fell off my chair when I saw myself popping out of the bushes, and acting like a half-pint Bigfoot.

The part where that big Bigfoot appeared was a heart stopper. The cameraman stopped the projector so everyone could look a long time at that Bigfoot. There was a lot of gasping and whispering going on. Then the film started rolling again, and showed our class marching out of the forest to board the bus. From here on the pictures were new to all the kids. The camera zoomed from us around to where the big Bigfoot had showed itself. The bushes shook, and Bigfoot showed its face again. And then one hairy hand started peeling a mask off its face. There was Sara, grinning and laughing. She waved. The cameraman then showed her pulling the top of the costume off her hands and arms, and over her head. That ended the picture.

Now I held my breath. I was afraid someone would say something to hurt Sara's feelings. Instead, everyone cheered and clapped, and Sara had to take a bow. After she did that, she hauled me off my seat and told everyone, "Thank my boy, Joey. It was all his idea."

I took a bow.

Mr. Nelson asked the cameraman to run the film again. He did. It was even better the second time. Afterwards the mothers served refreshments. A lot of people admitted to Sara that they believed in Bigfoot, but never before had the nerve to say so. That made her feel good. Some even asked her to keep on searching for Bigfoot. If anyone deserved credit for solving the mystery about the monster, she sure did. Sara promised she would keep looking, now that she had me to help.

So, now you know the whole story from the beginning to the end. Except . . .

Sara and I still spend weekends and summers looking for the real Bigfoot. I have a camera now. I always take it with me. Maybe someday my pictures will tell the world the truth about Bigfoot.

You'd like that, wouldn't you?

THE AUTHOR

MARIAN T. PLACE, the author of over forty books for children and young people, specializes in the American West and is the recipient of four Golden Spur Awards given by the Western Writers of America for Best Western juvenile novel and Best Western juvenile nonfiction title. She has worked as a newspaperwoman and a children's librarian, and has published over two hundred articles.

Her first book about North America's monster, *On the Track of Bigfoot*, won the 1977 Garden State Children's Book Award. She has also written a second nonfiction volume, *Bigfoot All Over the Country*, and a novel entitled *Nobody Meets Bigfoot*.

Marian Place and her husband now live in Arizona but spend their summers touring Bigfoot Country in their travel trailer.